PUFFIN BOOKS

EDDIE AND THE DIRTY DOGS

Herbie Brennan is the author of more than seventy books for children and adults, including the best-selling *Grailquest* series. He and his wife live in Ireland, where their lives are ruled by a cat called Cutipus Rex and five of his relations who keep all the ducks at a distance.

Herbie Brennan
Eddie and the Dirty Dogs

Illustrated by Ann Kronheimer

PUFFIN BOOKS

*For Tina and Noreen who
pulled the Rug through*

PUFFIN BOOKS

Published by the Penguin Group
Penguin Books Ltd, 27 Wrights Lane, London W8 5TZ, England
Penguin Putnam Inc., 375 Hudson Street, New York, New York 10014, USA
Penguin Books Australia Ltd, Ringwood, Victoria, Australia
Penguin Books Canada Ltd, 10 Alcorn Avenue, Toronto, Ontario, Canada M4V 3B2
Penguin Books (NZ) Ltd, Private Bag 102902, NSMC, Auckland, New Zealand

On the World Wide Web at: www.penguin.com

Penguin Books Ltd, Registered Offices: Harmondsworth, Middlesex, England

First published 2001
1 3 5 7 9 10 8 6 4 2

Text copyright © Herbie Brennan, 2001
Illustrations copyright © Ann Kronheimer, 2001
All rights reserved

The moral right of the author and illustrator has been asserted

Printed in Hong Kong by Midas Printing Ltd

British Library Cataloguing in Publication Data
A CIP catalogue record for this book is available from the British Library

ISBN 0–141–30778–1

··· Contents ···

1. Paws for Thought   1

2. Goatnapped   5

3. Handsome Ransom   9

4. In the Doghouse   15

5. Dopey Duck   21

6. Anvil Chorus   27

7. Poor Poodle   33

8. Big Entrance   37

9. Countdown   43

10. Duck on a Roll   49

11. Duck in the Drink   53

··· Chapter One ···
Paws for Thought

My name is Eddie. I'm a duck. It was a slow day at my ducktective office and a hot day in the city. I went for a swim.

As I climbed from the pond, a French poodle threw me a piece of bread. "Thanks, ma'am," I said. In this life you take what you can get.

Especially on a slow day.

"You are Eddie ze Duck, no?" she asked.

"Yes, ma'am." I nodded. I handed her my card. It said:

Eddie's Ducktective Agency

316, Downtown

"We Never Duck the Tough Jobs"

"My name is Fifi Bernard. Shall we – how you say? – shake a paw?"

I shook her paw, which isn't easy for a duck. "How can I help you, ma'am?" I asked.

She was wearing a black dress, black shoes and a black hat with a black veil.

She looked at me and burst into tears, which is an effect I sometimes have on dames. "I 'ave just lost my 'usband, Monsieur Eddie," she said.

"Sorry for your trouble, ma'am." I put a wing around her shoulder.

"I want you to find him for me," she sniffed.

"Better tell me all about it, ma'am," I said.

··· Chapter Two ···
Goatnapped

Fifi pulled out a handkerchief and dabbed her eyes. "This morning I went off to poodle round the mall. When I came back my beloved 'usband, he was gone. He would never leave me so I think he may 'ave been – how do you say? – goatnapped!"

"Kidnapped, ma'am," I corrected her.

Fifi Bernard ignored me. "Will you help me, Eddie ze Duck?"

"That's what I do, ma'am," I said. "What is your husband's name, ma'am?"

"Saint," she told me. "He's a dachshund."

"Saint Bernard," I mused. "Odd name for a dachshund, ma'am."

She laid a paw on my wing. "Eddie –" She hesitated. "May I call you Eddie?"

"Yes, ma'am," I said.

She had big brown eyes. Now she opened them very wide. "Eddie," she said, "please bring my beloved 'usband back to me."

"I'll try, ma'am," I said. "If you hear from the kidnappers, call me at the phone number on the card."

She frowned. "There is no phone number on this card."

"Sorry, ma'am," I said. "I guess I'll just have to call you."

She wrote her number and home address on the back of a dog biscuit and handed it across. "That's to keep you going, Eddie," she said and kissed me on the cheek. Before I could recover, she had disappeared across the park.

I was relieved to see her go. It meant I could stop saying *ma'am*.

··· Chapter Three ···
Handsome Ransom

The phone was ringing as I got back to the office. Since my girl, Gloria, had long since gone home, I grabbed it myself. It was Fifi Bernard.

"How did you get my number, Fif?" I asked.

"I rang Duckrectory Inquiries,"

she said. "But that is not important.
The goatnappers 'ave called me.
They want a ransom of two
thousand unmarked dog biscuits
before they will return my beloved
'usband to me."

I whistled softly, which isn't easy
for a duck. Two thousand biscuits
was a lot of chow, even for a Saint

Bernard. "Can you come up with that much?" I asked. Anybody who had two thousand biscuits in the bank had to be really loaded.

"I 'ave them here," Fifi said. "But Eddie, these dirty dogs wish me to deliver it to a hideout in the woods many miles from the city and I am fearful."

"Have you called the cops?" I asked.

Fifi sounded close to tears. "I am fearful of that too. They said if I called ze policemen they would shoot my beloved 'usband with their splurge guns. It would take him weeks to get the paint off."

OK, so the cops were out of it. "Leave this to me, babe," I said. "Pack the biscuits in a bright yellow suitcase, then wait."

"What are you going to do, Eddie?"

"Deliver the ransom and catch the kidnappers," I told her. "That's what you're paying me for."

"Oh, Eddie, you are my 'ero!" Fifi exclaimed.

I blushed and set the phone down. Then I checked her address on the back of my biscuit and set off into the night.

··· Chapter Four ···
In the Doghouse

Fifi lived in a large, expensive kennel on the west side. But as I swung the duckmobile into her driveway, I noticed the walls could do with a fresh coat of paint.

She was waiting for me at the doorway. She threw her paws around me and licked my face.

"I am so 'appy to see you!" she exclaimed. "I just know you are going to solve all my problems!"

I wriggled free and brushed down my feathers, then followed her into the kennel. The furniture had hairs all over it. "Have you got the biscuits?"

She pointed to a suitcase on the table. "It's all there – every crumb. Do you wish to count it?"

I shook my head. "Leave that to the bad guys. Where is this supposed to be delivered?"

"The delivery address is on the label."

I looked at the label. It said:

The Hideout
The Woods
Far From
The City

That was good enough for me. I turned to Fifi. "OK," I said. "I want you to stay here and stay close to the phone."

"What is your plan, Eddie?" she asked.

I shrugged. "I leave the suitcase where they said. Then I hide and watch it. When the bad guys come to collect the case I jump them."

Her eyes were bright. "Will you make them tell you where they 'ave hid my 'usband?"

"Sure I will," I said. I just hoped they weren't rotweilers.

She handed me a bottle of swamp water. "I thought you might need this to warm you up," she said.

"Thanks, babe," I said. I grabbed the bottle and the suitcase and headed for the woods.

··· Chapter Five ···
Dopey Duck

The duckmobile ate up the miles as I left the city. I ate up a take-out birdseed from my local greasy spoon, washed down with Fifi's swamp water. I didn't want to face the bad guys on an empty stomach.

The suitcase was sitting on the

passenger seat beside me. The yellow leather glinted in the headlights every time there was a passing car. It was my colour.

I checked the glove compartment for my splurge gun, but it was full of gloves. I shrugged. I would just have to do without it.

Soon the city lights were far

behind. Miles out, I saw the turn-off
I'd been waiting for. The road sign
said:

To the Woods
To the Woods

I figured I must be seeing double,
but there was nothing I could do
about it. I swung the duckmobile on

to the side-road and minutes later
I was driving through the woods.
All I needed was to find the hideout.

But suddenly my eyesight started
getting worse. The trees looked
funny in the headlights, like they
were giant people reaching out to
grab me. I was feeling sleepy.
Sleepy. Sleeeeeepy ... the word
echoed in my skull.

It made no sense to keep on
driving, so I pulled in to the side to
try to clear my head. I felt like I'd
been doped. But how? All I'd eaten
was the birdseed.

Then it hit me. "Fifi's swamp
water!" I exclaimed aloud.

"Right," growled a quiet voice
behind me.

I turned to see a dark shape climbing up from the floor of the car. It was a dachshund carrying a splurge gun. He poked it in my ear, which is hard to find on a duck. He gave me a lopsided grin. "Nice to meet you, Eddie – I'm Saint Bernard."

"What are you doing in my car?" I asked. But I didn't really care. Before he got around to answering, I passed out.

··· Chapter Six ···
Anvil Chorus

I woke up feeling like my head was packed with blacksmiths, all using my brain for an anvil.

"Oooooh!" I said.

I tried to move, but couldn't, on account of somebody having wrapped me up with sticky tape. My head poked out, but otherwise

I thought I was back in the egg.

There was a noise behind me. I looked round. Which was peculiar because I usually look square.

There was something white and blurred in front of me. After a while it swam into focus. It was Fifi with a frisbee in her mouth. "What's a nice dog like you doing in a dump like this?" I asked.

"Waiting for you to wake up," she said. "And playing with this frisbee."

I would have shrugged if I could have, but I couldn't, so I didn't. I just blinked casually instead. I seemed to be in some sort of cabin in the woods. "I'm awake as it gets," I said.

She came over close to me. "Oh, Eddie," she said, "I didn't know it would be like this now."

"Didn't know what would be like what when?" I asked, wondering what I was talking about. The blacksmiths in my head were on

their tea break, but even so it was hard to think.

She pulled a hankie from her handbag and dabbed at a spot of mud on her front paw. That's when I knew she was going to come clean.

"I will tell you everything," she said. "I owe you that much before …"

"Before?" I echoed.

"Before we set the splurge bomb," she told me.

··· Chapter Seven ···
Poor Poodle

"My beloved Saint and I had problems," Fifi explained. "Our kennel is in an expensive part of town and Saint likes to eat out a lot."

"So you ran short of cash?" I said.

She nodded. "Yes."

I sniffed, which isn't easy for a duck. Especially one that's wrapped in sticky tape. "If you're so short of cash, how come you raised two thousand dog biscuits?" I asked sourly.

"There were never any biscuits," Fifi said. The yellow suitcase was on the chair beside her. She flipped it open. Inside there was nothing but old newspapers cut to look like biscuits.

She closed the case. "When the money started to run out Saint thought up a plan."

"Which was?" I asked. But deep inside I knew.

Fifi looked sheepish, which is a great trick for a poodle. "That we sell you to Mr Big. He's on his way here now."

It made sense. Mr Big wanted me bad because I'd put so many of his men in jail.

"You'll never get away with this," I said. It was a line I'd heard in a movie, but somehow it didn't sound convincing now.

"But I think I will," said Fifi. She threw the frisbee through the door and chased it.

Leaving me alone to wait for Mr Big.

··· Chapter Eight ···
Big Entrance

I hadn't long to wait. Less than thirty seconds later, Saint Bernard walked in with Mr Big. I recognized him at once because he was so small.

"Hi, Eddie," he nodded. "Nice to see my friends have got you taped."

"The pleasure's all yours," I wisequacked sourly.

Saint was carrying a large can of bright, passionate-pink dye and a black box that trailed electric wires. "What's your toy, Saint Bernard?" I asked quickly.

PERMANENT
THIS COLOUR
PINK DYE
LASTS FOREVER

"It's not a toy Saint Bernard," Mr Big put in. "It's a splurge bomb."

Saint gave me a devilish grin. "Once I wire up this baby your goose is cooked, duck. The dye is indelible. It will never wash out however many ponds you jump in. You'll be the world's first dyed duck, permanent, pure, passionate pink!"

I closed my eyes in horror. It was the end of a promising career. Nobody would take a passionate-pink ducktective seriously.

"You'll never get away with this," I said again. It didn't sound any more convincing the second time.

They both ignored me. Mr Big watched while Saint Bernard wired the can of dye to the black box. Then he carried the contraption across the room and set it on the table beside me.

"Have to make sure you get a good view, duck." He grinned.

He flipped a switch on the side of the box. At once it began to tick. A panel on the front lit up. On it were the words:

YOU WILL BE SPLURGED IN
4 MINUTES AND 59 SECONDS ...
AND COUNTING!

"OK, boss," Saint Bernard said. "Let's get outside before this thing blows."

"Bye, bye, Eddie," Mr Big said. "You'll be in the pink next time we meet."

Together they ran from the cabin. The panel on the front of the box now read:

YOU WILL BE SPLURGED IN
4 MINUTES AND 29 SECONDS ...
AND COUNTING!

··· Chapter Nine ···
Countdown

I did what any duck would do. I panicked. Saint Bernard and Mr Big had only been gone thirty seconds and already the panel was reading:

YOU WILL BE SPLURGED IN
3 MINUTES AND 59 SECONDS ...
AND COUNTING!

Then I got it together and started to think. The dirty dogs had left the cabin door ajar in their hurry to get out. But that was no good to me. When you're wrapped in sticky tape from neck to foot you can't make a run for it.

And since my wings were taped on to my sides, there was no way I could fly.

YOU WILL BE SPLURGED IN
3 MINUTES AND 28 SECONDS ...
AND COUNTING

Couldn't run. Couldn't fly. Couldn't do anything except sit there wrapped up like a beach ball in the sticky tape and wait for the splurge bomb to make me a pink duck.

I closed my eyes and tried to think even harder. After a while I opened them again.

YOU WILL BE SPLURGED IN
2 MINUTES AND 57 SECONDS ...
AND COUNTING!

There had to be something I could do. I went over it one more time. Couldn't run. Couldn't fly. Couldn't ...

YOU WILL BE SPLURGED IN
1 MINUTE AND 30 SECONDS ...
AND COUNTING

A light bulb went on inside my head. I could roll! If I could just fall over, I could roll! I started to rock backwards and forwards.

But I could see the words on the little screen:

YOU WILL BE SPLURGED IN
0 MINUTES AND 29 SECONDS ...
AND COUNTING!

The ticking seemed to be getting louder. I rocked harder. 20 seconds ... 15 seconds ... 10 seconds ...

It was too late. The splurge bomb was about to blow!

··· Chapter Ten ···
Duck on a Roll

I tipped over and started to roll. The floor must have been on a slope because I rolled faster and faster. I hit the door as the splurge bomb blew. A splat of dye struck me, but it missed my head, so it was only the sticky tape turned pink.

Suddenly I was outside, rolling faster than ever. The world spun around me in a jumble of trees and grass and ground. The cabin was built on a height, so I was rolling like a rocket now.

"He is getting – how you say? – away!" I heard Fifi Bernard scream.

"Stop him!" ordered Mr Big.

I could see them lining up to grab me, but I couldn't stop rolling.

"I'll get him!" shouted Saint Bernard. He ran to stand directly in my path, arms outstretched.

I hit him like a bowling ball and he went over like a nine-pin. "Ooow-wow-wow-wow!" he howled as he landed in a thorn bush. I saw him struggling to get out, but the thorns held him fast.

"Leave him to me!" called Fifi, leaping out in front of me.

She went down even faster than her husband, right into the same thorn bush. She thrashed round vainly trying to get out. "Help!" she shouted. "You must help me, Eddie! I have suddenly fallen in love with you!"

I was rolling so fast now that when I hit Mr Big he spun high into the air. A tree branch caught under his collar and he hung there, high up off the ground, his legs kicking helplessly. "Get me down!" he ordered. "Get me down!"

But I had problems of my own. I was rolling straight towards a river.

··· Chapter Eleven ···
Duck in the Drink

Can a duck swim without his feet to paddle? Can a duck float when he's wrapped in bright pink sticky tape? Will the bad guys win this time? Does anybody care?

But I had no time for questions. I hit the water rolling. I rolled straight across the river and out the other side.

I rolled up the far bank, slowed, stopped, then started to roll back. I gathered speed. I rolled into the river. It was starting to feel familiar.

This time I stayed there. The current carried me downstream a little way before I became wedged between two rocks. Fortunately my head was above water.

It was a relief to stop rolling and good not to be drowning, but what was I going to do? I was still wrapped like a parcel, couldn't move my feet or wings and now I was stuck fast between two rocks in a river.

I wondered if I could train a fish
to pull off sticky tape.

I was still wondering when I
realized I wouldn't have to. The
river water was softening the glue
on the tape. It was starting to
unwrap and float around me like a
passionate-pink cloud.

In a minute I could move my feet. A minute more and I was stretching my wings. I shook free of the last of the tape and paddled for the shore. Mr Big and Saint and Fifi were still stuck fast.

"Let me down!" screamed Mr Big.

"Get us out!" shouted Fifi and Saint.

I gave them all a cheery wave. Then I waddled off to find a phone box where I could call the cops.

"You OK, Eddie?" asked the sergeant when I made the call.

"Nearly dyed," I said. "But now I'm in the pink."